Jasmine Green
Rescues
A Piglet
Called Truffle

Helen Peters
illustrated by Ellie Snowdon

WALKER BOOKS

For Dorothea
H. P.

For my family
E. S.

First U.S. edition 2020
First published by Nosy Crow (U.K.) 2016

Library of Congress Catalog Card Number pending
ISBN 978-1-5362-1024-8 (hardcover)
ISBN 978-1-5362-1459-8 (paperback)

20 21 22 23 24 25 TRC 10 9 8 7 6 5 4 3 2 1

Printed in Eagan, MN, U.S.A.

This book was typeset in Bembo.
The illustrations were done in pencil with a digital wash overlay.

Walker Books US
a division of
Candlewick Press
99 Dover Street
Somerville, Massachusetts 02144

www.walkerbooksus.com

Read all the books in the
JASMINE GREEN RESCUES series

Truffle found this way

Oak Tree Farm

← **Willow found this way**

← To village and school

Tom's house

To Mrs. Thomas's house
& Angus Mizon's farm

South
Towns

river

Ben's
house

Button
found here

Sky
found here

Chicken coop

Farmyard

Holly
found here

Jasmine's
house

Calf barn

Lucky
born here

To Roger Turner's farm →

1
You Poor Little Thing

Jasmine was lying on her bed with her cats, reading her favorite magazine, *Practical Pigs*. It was a Friday afternoon in late November, and Jasmine, absorbed in an interesting article about rare breeds, was completely happy.

"Jasmine!" called her mom up the stairs. "I have to go to a calving at Carter's. Do you want to come?"

Jasmine swung her feet to the floor. Mr. Carter was a grumpy old farmer with a permanent scowl on his face, but he kept pigs, and that was reason enough to visit his farm. Jasmine's dad was a farmer, too, and he kept plenty of calves. But, despite Jasmine's constant pleading, there were no pigs at Oak Tree Farm.

"I'll be back soon," Jasmine murmured to the cats, stroking the tops of their heads. "Have a lovely sleep."

Marmite purred as Jasmine stroked her thick black fur. Toffee lay curled up on a blanket at the end of the bed, and didn't open his eyes as Jasmine left the room.

Jasmine's mom, Nadia, was standing at the bottom of the stairs in her coat and boots, jingling her keys like she always did when she was impatient.

"Come on, Jas. Grab your coat, I need to go."

As a farm vet, Mom often got called out at inconvenient times. Jasmine sometimes thought farmers purposely waited until mealtimes to make their emergency phone calls to the vet.

Jasmine pulled her muddy waterproof jacket from its hook by the Aga stove in the kitchen. Her older sister, Ella, sat at the kitchen table, frowning over a textbook. The table was covered with schoolbooks and files and scraps of paper and pens.

"We shouldn't be too long," Mom said to Ella. "I've put some baked potatoes in the Aga."

"Uh-huh," said Ella vaguely. She didn't look up from her books.

Jasmine and Mom walked out into the front garden, past the kennel where Bramble, the old springer spaniel, lived.

The kennel always made Jasmine sad these days. Until last month, there had been two dogs living there. But Bramble's sister, Bracken, had died of old age a month ago, and now Bramble was on her own. It must be so strange and lonely for her, Jasmine thought.

At the moment, the kennel was empty. Bramble was out in the fields with Jasmine's dad.

Mom opened the gate. "Manu, Ben, I'm going out on a call," she hollered into the tangle of bushes at the edge of the farmyard.

There was a rustling noise, and two mud-smeared faces poked out through the damp twigs.

One belonged to Jasmine's five-year-old brother, Manu, and the other to his best friend, Ben, who lived in the house at the end of the farm road.

"Do you want some of our crumble?" asked Manu. He thrust a plastic tub through the leaves.

"What sort of crumble?" asked Mom.

Jasmine peered into the tub.

"Mud crumble, it looks like. With a crunchy dead-leaf topping."

"It's got yew berries and acorns in it, too," said Ben.

"It's dying crumble," said Manu.

"Dying crumble?" asked Mom.

"Yes," said Manu. "If you eat it, you die."

"It sounds lovely," said Mom, "but I think I'll pass. Daddy's checking the sheep in the Thirteen Acres and Ella's inside if you need anything."

"OK," said Manu.

"Thank you, Dr. Singh," said Ben. He was always super polite to adults. That was how he got away with being so naughty.

"And don't eat that crumble," called Mom.

"No, Dr. Singh, we won't," said Ben. "Thank you, Dr. Singh. Bye, Dr. Singh." And their heads disappeared back into the bushes.

Mr. Carter appeared from a cowshed as they drove into the farmyard. He was a stocky, middle-aged man in a dirty waterproof coat and baggy overalls tucked into enormous black boots. As always, he had a scowl on his face.

"Afternoon, Jim," said Mom, getting out of the car.

Mr. Carter didn't return the greeting. "Breech birth, I reckon," he grunted as Mom opened the trunk of the car and took out her cases of medicine and equipment. "Been straining for hours."

"Can I go see the pigs?" asked Jasmine.

Mr. Carter gave a grunt, which Jasmine took as a yes. She was halfway across the yard when he called, "There's a sow just farrowed. Eleven, she's had."

Jasmine gave a squeal of delight. Newborn piglets!

"Watch out for that old sow, though," called the farmer.

"And disinfect your boots first," said Mom. "Here," she said, taking from the trunk a plastic bucket containing a bottle of disinfectant and a scrubbing brush.

Jasmine took the bucket and filled it from the tap in the milking parlor. She poured disinfectant in, carried the bucket back to the yard, and handed the scrubbing brush to her mother. Mom scrubbed her boots and passed the brush to Jasmine, who did the same. It was one of those boring jobs that had to be done, like brushing your teeth. "We can't risk spreading infections between farms," Mom always said.

Now that her boots were thoroughly disinfected, Jasmine splashed through the muddy puddles to the pigsties. Every sty had a stable door. The bottom halves were bolted shut, but the top halves were open.

7

Jasmine leaned over the half door of the first sty and peered in. It was empty. The second sty contained one old sow lying asleep on a pile of straw. But there were rustling and grunting noises coming from the third one.

Jasmine looked in. A sleek pig lay on her side in a bed of straw. Sucking busily at her long double line of teats was a row of silky little newborn piglets, pink with black splotches. Their tiny curly tails wriggled with delight as they drank their mother's milk.

Jasmine grinned at the scene. "You," she said to the piglets, "are so lovely. And you," she told the sow, "are very clever."

Even though Mr. Carter had already told her there were eleven piglets, Jasmine couldn't resist counting the row of little bodies packed tightly together.

Yes, there were eleven.

But then something caught her attention. At the far end of the row, from underneath the biggest and fattest piglet in the litter, there was a movement in the straw. A rustling sort of movement.

Was it a mouse?

Jasmine looked more closely. There was another movement, and she saw a little patch of pink beneath the straw.

Jasmine tugged at the bolt on the sty door. It didn't budge. She wriggled and pulled and gradually inched it back until, with a final jerk, it came free. She stepped inside the sty and leaned over the door to bolt it shut again. The pigs didn't look like they were planning to escape, but you could never be sure.

"It's all right," Jasmine reassured the sow. "I've just come to look."

Slowly and quietly, so as not to disturb the feeding babies or alarm the new mother, she crept along the row to where the biggest piglet was feeding, tucked just in front of the sow's hind legs. Yes, there was definitely something underneath it, almost buried in the straw.

Jasmine crouched down. Gently she lifted the warm, soft body of the biggest piglet. It squealed indignantly, and the mother raised her head and

bared her yellow teeth with a low growl. Jasmine hastily laid the piglet next to another teat.

The sow laid down her head again, alarm over. Jasmine gently parted the straw where the big piglet had been lying.

There, shivering convulsively, lay the smallest piglet Jasmine had ever seen.

It was about half the size of the others, and not much bigger than Jasmine's hand. It clearly didn't have the strength to push its way through its brothers and sisters to get a drink.

"Oh," she said. "Oh, you poor little thing."

She scooped up the trembling runt, feeling the bones beneath its thin skin. It didn't make a sound. She picked off the pieces of straw from around its mouth and snout, and laid it gently in front of a free teat. Its wet little snout was touching the teat, but the piglet didn't open its mouth. Its tiny tail hung limp and straight.

It must be too weak to feed, she thought. She had to tell Mr. Carter straightaway. He had said there were eleven piglets. So he hadn't seen the runt.

"Don't worry," she murmured to the tiny pig. "I'm going to get help."

2

The Scrawniest Runt I've Ever Seen

Jasmine left the sty, bolting the door after her. There was no time to lose. At any moment, the little piglet might get trampled and crushed by the others.

The farmer was striding toward the sties, pushing a wheelbarrow containing a bucket of pig feed.

"Mr. Carter," said Jasmine, "did you know there are actually twelve piglets in that new litter?"

Mr. Carter grunted. "Eleven."

"I thought there were eleven, too, but then I saw

there was a tiny little runt underneath the others. They were sitting on top of it and it couldn't feed. I put it right by the teats, but I think it's too weak to suck."

Mr. Carter grunted. "It'll have to take its chances. I haven't got the time to see to it, and there's nobody else around."

Jasmine stared at him, outraged. How could he be so uncaring?

"But it will die if nobody helps it."

The farmer peered through the door of the sty at the newborn litter. He whistled. "That's the scrawniest runt I've ever seen. It'll never survive. Should put it out of its misery."

"Kill it?" Jasmine shrieked. "No! You can't do that!"

Mr. Carter picked up a battered shovel that was leaning against the wall, threw it into the wheelbarrow, and opened the door of the middle sty. He pushed the wheelbarrow inside. The old sow heaved herself to her feet.

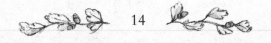

Jasmine thought fast. She knew her parents wouldn't approve, but they wouldn't want the poor little pig to die, would they?

She plucked up her courage. "Would you let me take the piglet?" she asked. "I could look after it and then bring it back when it's stronger."

Mr. Carter scowled as he tipped the bucket of meal into the sow's trough. A floury cloud rose all around him. "Wouldn't do any good. It would smell different from the others when it came back. The sow would reject it and the young ones would bully it."

"Well, could I just keep it, then?"

Mr. Carter snorted. "Don't be daft. What do you know about pigs?"

"I could learn. I read *Practical Pigs*."

Mr. Carter gave a laugh that was worse than his snort. "It hasn't got a chance, that one. Survival of the fittest, that's what it is. Nature's way."

He pushed the wheelbarrow to the far corner of the sty and began to shovel up the muck.

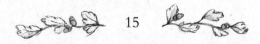

Jasmine stood in the yard, scowling at the farmer's back. With any luck, he would trip and fall headfirst into his dung-filled wheelbarrow.

Mom emerged from the cowshed, peeling off the long plastic disposable gloves she wore for calvings. She smiled at Jasmine.

"That was a lot easier than I feared," she said. "Lovely little bull calf. Ready to go?"

No, Jasmine thought. *I'm not ready to go. I can't leave that pig to die.*

"I'm just going to say goodbye to the piglets," she said.

"All right, but hurry up. I need to get home and make dinner."

"I'll be really quick. I just have to do one thing."

If the pig had started to suck, Jasmine thought, then she wouldn't need to do anything. But if it hadn't, then surely it would be cruel to walk away and leave the poor creature to the mercies of Mr. Carter.

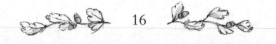

She leaned over the door of the sty. The little runt was where she had left it, lying on top of two of the others, eyes closed, violently trembling. Its snout brushed the mother's teat but it made no attempt to suck.

Jasmine took a look around. Mom was loading her medicine and equipment into the trunk of the car. "Come and scrub your boots, Jasmine," she called.

It wouldn't be worth asking Mom, Jasmine decided. She probably wouldn't approve of taking an animal from a farmer without permission. She might even use a word like "stealing." And there was no time for useless arguments. Already the poor little pig looked as if it hardly had any life left in it.

Jasmine opened the door of the sty and tiptoed inside. Gently, she slipped one hand underneath the piglet's head and the other under its shivering back. It was almost all pink, but it had a few black spots on its back. It was not much larger than a guinea pig.

"I don't know if you're a boy or a girl," she whispered, "but I think you're a girl. I'm going to call you Truffle."

Truffle kept her eyes closed and made no

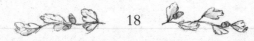

sound as Jasmine lifted her up and slipped her inside her coat. She was so small that she hardly made a bulge.

"Please don't die, Truffle," whispered Jasmine as she left the sty and bolted the door. "I'm going to look after you, I promise. Please just hang on until we get home and I'll make you all better."

With her right hand supporting the piglet inside her coat, Jasmine gave her boots a hasty

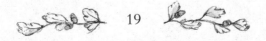

scrub. She emptied the bucket down a drain and shoved it back in the car.

"Ready?" called Mom, fastening her seat belt and starting the engine.

"Ready," said Jasmine. With one arm cradling the hidden piglet, she wrapped her coat around herself and carefully got into the car.

3

You'll Be Safe in Here

Back in her bedroom, Jasmine emptied the bag full of straw she had collected from her dad's barn into a cardboard box. She squeezed the box into the space between her bed and the radiator. If anyone came in, the bed should shield the box from sight. She was relieved to see the cats had left the room. She wasn't sure what they would make of this new animal.

She unzipped her jacket and lifted out the tiny pig. Truffle's eyes were still closed and her breathing was rapid and shallow.

"I'm going to get you some food, Truffle," Jasmine whispered. "You'll be safe in here."

She lowered the piglet into the box. She had turned the radiator up to maximum and the room was warm, but Truffle was still shivering. Jasmine stroked her skinny back, ridged where the ribs stuck out.

"I'll be back in a minute. You just rest there and get your strength up."

She kissed the top of Truffle's head, straightened up, and ran downstairs. Ben and Manu stood at the kitchen table, stirring a hideous-looking concoction in a saucepan. The table was set for dinner, but there was no sign of Mom. She was probably in her office, catching up on paperwork, or on the phone with Jasmine's nani.

There was no sign of Ella, either. She must have retreated to her bedroom.

Jasmine walked over to the kettle and touched the side. It was warm, but not boiling. Perfect. She poured some of the water into a mug.

"Who do you think would win," Ben was saying, "in a fight between a bull and a polar bear?"

"Definitely the bull," said Manu. "Polar bears aren't even real."

"Of course they're real."

"How do you know? Have you ever seen one?"

"I've seen loads of photos," said Ben.

"But what if they're just drawings?"

"Of course they're not drawings. Anyway, there's lots of things that are real that you've never seen."

"Like what?"

"Like internal organs. Your heart and liver and stuff."

"I don't believe in internal organs," said Manu.

"How can you not believe in them? What do you think's inside you?"

"I don't know. I've never seen inside me."

"But scientists know they exist."

"They could be lying," said Manu.

Jasmine took the mug of warm water into the

mudroom next to the kitchen and reached up to the wall cupboard where her parents kept the farm medicine.

Please let there be some colostrum in here, she thought.

She had no experience with pigs, but she had bottle-fed plenty of sickly newborn lambs, and it was vital that they were given colostrum. Colostrum, the mother's first milk, contained a lot of protein, as well as antibodies to protect newborn animals from disease. Truffle had missed out on that from her mother, and Jasmine was desperate to find a packet of colostrum powder in the medicine cupboard.

The cupboard had a padlock, but she knew the combination. She started sorting through the dozens of medicine bottles and boxes of tablets with their printed labels. Right at the back, behind an assortment of syringes, was an individual packet of colostrum substitute.

"Yes!" she whispered triumphantly, pulling it

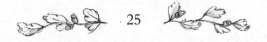

out and stuffing it in her coat pocket. She locked the medicine cupboard and opened the cupboard under the sink, where her dad kept the things for the bottle-fed lambs. Jasmine pulled out a rubber teat and a feeding bottle with measurements marked on the side. She stuffed them in her other coat pocket. *Luckily my coat has such nice big pockets,* she thought.

Then she picked up the mug and went back to her bedroom.

She peered into the box. Truffle was shaking convulsively, almost as though she was having a fit.

"Hello, little one," Jasmine whispered, stroking the piglet's shivering back. "I'm going to feed you now, and then you'll feel better."

She set the mug down on the bedside table, sat on the bed, and took the things from her coat pockets. She unscrewed the top of the bottle and tore the packet open. She tipped the powder into the bottle and read the instructions on the back

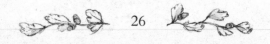

of the packet. Then she carefully added the correct amount of warm water.

The instructions said you should whisk the powder into the water for three minutes to get smooth milk with no lumps. But Jasmine didn't have a whisk, and she wasn't about to make another trip downstairs and risk awkward questions. So she pinched the teat tightly between her thumb and forefinger and then shook the bottle vigorously, timing it on her bedside clock.

Three minutes of vigorously shaking a bottle felt like a very long time.

When the shaking was done, she pulled up the sleeve of her sweater and shook a few drops of the thick, yellowy mixture onto her wrist to make sure it was at body temperature. If the milk felt either hot or cold on the thin skin of

her wrist, that would mean it wasn't the right temperature.

The milk felt just right. Finally, everything was ready.

Along the landing, she heard Mom scrape her desk chair back and call, "Jasmine! Dinnertime!"

Oh, no.

If she went down to dinner now, it would be at least another half hour before Truffle was fed. And that half hour could be the difference between life and death.

4

A Tiny Bit at a Time

Jasmine put the bottle on the floor beside Truffle's box and left the room, closing the door behind her. She couldn't risk Mom coming in.

"Oh, there you are," said Mom. "Come down to dinner. You must be starving."

"I'm not hungry at all," Jasmine lied. "I can't eat any dinner. I . . . I feel really sick."

Mom raised her eyebrows. "Have you been eating sweets from Nani in your room again?"

"No," said Jasmine indignantly. "I don't even have any sweets."

"Hmm," said Mom. She put her palm to Jasmine's forehead and looked closely at her face. "You seem all right. Come down to dinner and try to eat, at least. It's only baked potatoes."

"I can't," said Jasmine, pressing a hand to her stomach and wincing. "My tummy feels really funny. Can I just lie down in bed?"

Mom looked surprised. "Really? Well, I'd better bring you up a bucket, then, in case you get sick."

"It's OK, I've already got one," said Jasmine quickly. The last thing she wanted was Mom coming into her room.

"Oh, good girl." Mom kissed the top of her head. "Go on, then, just lie down and rest. Call me if you need me."

Mom walked down the landing and knocked on Ella's door. "Ella! Dinnertime!"

Jasmine hurried back to her room. She felt bad about deceiving Mom, but a life was at stake here.

She bent down, lifted the trembling pig out of

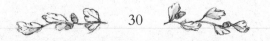

30

the box, and laid her in her lap. Gently, she held the bottle to her mouth. Truffle didn't respond. Jasmine held it there patiently, but the piglet's mouth stayed shut. She slipped her fingers into Truffle's mouth and prized her jaw open. It was remarkably resistant, and she was surprised to feel a row of sharp little teeth.

She pushed the teat in, but it slipped right out again. She

tried several times, but Truffle made no attempt to suck. She clearly had no strength at all.

Sometimes, the weakest lambs were like this. She would have to fetch a feeding syringe from the medicine cupboard.

Everybody else was in the kitchen, eating dinner. If she didn't want to be seen, she would have to go by the outside route.

Jasmine tiptoed downstairs and softly opened the front door. She went out into the cold November night, closing the door behind her as quietly as she could. Then she walked around the side of the house. Luckily, the back door was kept unlocked until Dad bolted it before he went to bed.

Jasmine held her breath as she opened it. "Please don't creak," she whispered.

It wouldn't have mattered if the door had creaked. The kitchen was full of noise, with the radio on in the background and Manu and Ben in peals of laughter. Nobody would have heard the back door opening.

Jasmine unlocked the cupboard and reached for a syringe. A medicine bottle toppled over and clattered onto the tiled floor. Jasmine held her breath. But the noise in the kitchen carried on. She put the bottle back in the cupboard and, standing on tiptoe, carefully extracted a feeding syringe, wrapped in its sterile plastic packaging. She put it in her pocket. Then she tiptoed outside, walked around to the front door, reentered the house, and went back to her bedroom.

Truffle was still trembling, and now there was drool coming out of her mouth, too. That was a bad sign. Jasmine would have to work fast.

She unscrewed the top of the feeding bottle and dipped the nozzle of the syringe into the colostrum. She pulled back the plunger, and the syringe filled with the rich, creamy mixture.

Jasmine sat on the edge of the bed and gently lifted the pig onto her lap, talking softly to her the whole time.

"Now, Truffle," she said, prizing her jaw open

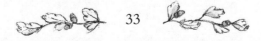

and slipping the little plastic nozzle into her mouth, "can you swallow this for me? No need to suck, I'm just going to drop it down your throat, a tiny bit at a time. OK?"

To Jasmine's relief, the milk, drop by drop, seemed to actually be going down Truffle's throat. For a long time, Jasmine sat there, completely still, her world consisting only of the tiny mouth of a barely alive piglet.

If this didn't work, Jasmine thought, she would have to tell Mom. Her mom might be angry with her for stealing a pig, but she was a fantastic vet. She would do everything she could to keep Truffle alive. If she couldn't save Truffle, nobody could.

But Jasmine also knew that there was probably nothing Mom could do for Truffle that she herself wasn't already doing. Providing food and warmth was all anybody could do.

And then a miracle happened. The plunger had almost reached the bottom of the syringe when, suddenly, Truffle's eyes flickered open.

"Truffle!" Jasmine whispered. "Oh, Truffle, you're getting better!"

The little piglet had beautiful eyes. Deep, dark blue, with long sweeping lashes. But after a few seconds, they closed again.

"Open your eyes," Jasmine urged her. "Come on, Truffle, open your eyes."

But Truffle's eyes remained closed, and still she shivered.

"You need to be in the Aga, don't you," Jasmine said. "I'll put you in there once everyone's out of the kitchen."

The Aga had four separate ovens, two on each side, all permanently on at different temperatures. The one on the top right-hand side was really hot, but the one on the bottom left provided just a very gentle warmth, perfect for reviving sick baby animals. Dad often put orphaned lambs in the Aga, but it had never been used for a piglet before.

Suddenly a thought struck Jasmine. "I know. I'll get you a hot water bottle. Wait here a minute, and then I'll give you some more colostrum."

She put Truffle gently back in her box and packed straw all around her. Then she walked down to the kitchen. A hot water bottle was easy to explain. If anybody asked, it was to soothe her aching tummy.

Ben's mom was standing by the sink with a cup of tea, chatting to Jasmine's mom. Jasmine's dad

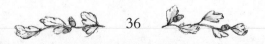

was standing with his back to the Aga, warming himself up after a day on the farm. Ben and Manu were still at the table, eating chocolate cookies.

"I hope these two behaved themselves today," Ben's mom said. "We don't want them getting sent to the principal twice in one week, do we?"

Jasmine's family, their eyes wide with shock, turned to Manu.

"You got sent to the *principal,* Manu?" asked Mom.

Perfect, thought Jasmine. Nobody would notice her now. She slipped behind them, took the kettle, filled it, and put it on the Aga's boiling plate.

"Oh, goodness, I'm sorry," said Ben's mom, looking really embarrassed. "I didn't realize you didn't know."

Jasmine might as well have been invisible. She took out her hot water bottle with the knitted cover from the cupboard under the sink.

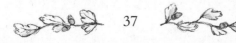

37

"You got sent to the *principal*?" said Ella. "In *kindergarten*? What did you do?"

"Not just us," said Manu. "Alfie and Noah, too."

"We didn't do anything wrong," said Ben. "It was just Alfie's sister making a fuss."

"What did you do?" asked Mom, giving Manu a hard stare.

"We were only playing Violent Babies," said Manu.

"Violent Babies?"

"It's this really good game Ben made up. We're all superheroes, but we're baby superheroes, so we can only crawl."

Ben grinned proudly. "We start in different corners of the playground, then we all crawl to the middle, and when we reach each other, we wrestle."

"It's a really good game," said Manu. "But Alfie's sister's such a spoilsport, she said we had to stop because we were frightening the preschoolers, and we didn't stop, so she told the really mean lunch lady."

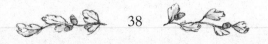

"The one with a face like a moldy turnip," said Ben.

"Ben!" said his mother.

"And the turnip lady sent us to the principal. And we hadn't done *anything*."

Everybody started talking at once. The kettle was nearly boiling. Jasmine filled the hot water bottle and slipped out of the kitchen.

5
I Won't Let You Die

Just before half past ten, Jasmine heard her mom walk up the stairs and go into the bathroom. Finally! She had been waiting all evening for her family to stop moving around.

She bent down and lifted Truffle out of her box. She had managed to get nearly all the colostrum down her during the evening, but Truffle was still shivering and breathing very fast. Jasmine tried to stand her up. She wobbled and collapsed back on her side.

Jasmine tried not to think depressing thoughts as she looked at the minuscule creature trembling in her lap. A night in the Aga would surely revive her, just as it had revived so many lambs over the years.

But not all of them.

Jasmine couldn't help thinking about Harry, her lamb from last spring. Harry had been barely alive when he was born. Dad had revived him three times in the Aga, but eventually he had died anyway.

"Sometimes, nature knows best," Dad had said. But Jasmine had been inconsolable for days.

What had Mr. Carter said? "Survival of the fittest."

Mom always said the first night was crucial for a newborn animal. If it was going to die, she would say, it would probably be dead by morning.

"You won't die," Jasmine whispered fiercely to Truffle. "You won't die because I won't let you die."

41

She took the fleecy blanket off the end of her bed and draped it over the little pig. The house seemed quiet, but you could never be sure. There had been a moment earlier when Mom had come into her room to see how she was feeling. Jasmine had thrown the blanket quickly over Truffle's box. "I was too hot with that thing on my bed," she said when Mom gave her a questioning look.

Cradling the blanket-covered Truffle in her arms, Jasmine crept out of her room, along the landing, and down the stairs.

A rustling noise came from the living room. Jasmine jumped and shrieked.

Dad appeared in the doorway, holding a copy of *Farmers Weekly*.

"Jasmine!" he exclaimed. "What on earth?"

"I thought you were in bed," said Jasmine.

"I thought *you* were in bed hours ago." He frowned at the blanket in her arms. "What are you doing?"

"It's . . . a surprise," Jasmine said. "For your birthday."

"My birthday? Well, that is a surprise. Seeing as my birthday isn't for another six months."

"I'm being prepared."

"Well, get back to bed now. You need your sleep."

"I'm just getting a glass of water," said Jasmine. "I won't be long."

"Hurry up, then, before you freeze." And he took his *Farmers Weekly* up to bed.

Jasmine went into the kitchen, turned on the light, and opened the bottom left-hand oven of the Aga. She took some old newspaper from the recycling box and laid it on the oven floor. Then she kissed the tiny piglet on the head and laid her on the newspaper.

"I'm going to leave the oven door ajar," she told Truffle, "and I'm going to come and feed you every single hour of the night. Don't worry one bit. You'll be safe in here. And I'll come and

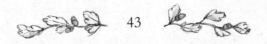

fetch you back up to my room very early in the morning, before anybody else gets up."

And then she went back to her room and set her alarm clock for one hour's time.

6
What Was That Noise?

Jasmine woke to the sound of shouting.

"Where are my soccer cleats?"

That was Manu, from the top of the stairs.

"Wherever you left them when you took them off."

That was Mom, from somewhere downstairs.

"Where's that?"

"Well, how would I know? They're your cleats."

Suddenly, Jasmine's stomach lurched. She sat bolt upright.

Truffle!

She had crept down and fed her every hour in the night. And she had meant to bring her back upstairs after her six o'clock feeding.

What time was it now?

She snatched her alarm clock from the bedside table.

Eight thirty! She had slept through her six o'clock alarm! And now everybody was up and Truffle was still in the Aga and how on earth was she going to smuggle her upstairs again before she was discovered?

Jasmine scrambled out of bed and ran downstairs in her bare feet. Mom was in the kitchen taking off her coat. She must have just gotten back from a call. She smiled as Jasmine came in.

"Have you just woken up? Oh, goodness, your feet will freeze. Go and put your slippers on."

"I'm not cold," said Jasmine. She had to check Truffle. At least nobody seemed to have discovered her yet.

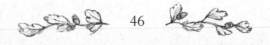

Mom went to fill the kettle. While her back was turned, Jasmine darted to the oven. She had her hand on the door when footsteps thundered down the stairs. Manu burst into the kitchen, pulled out a stool, and sat at the table facing the Aga.

"What do you think would kill you quicker, Jas, yew berries or rat poison?" he asked.

Jasmine didn't answer. This was terrible. How was she going to check on Truffle now? She didn't even know if she was still alive.

"It has to be yew," said Manu, who would settle for a conversation with himself if nobody else was willing to join in, "because rat poison is for killing rats, which are tiny, but yew kills massive animals like cows and horses."

Please be alive, Truffle, prayed Jasmine. *Please be alive.*

The back door opened and a gust of wind blew in through the mudroom. The door shut again and Jasmine heard Dad taking off his boots.

"Who'd like pancakes?" asked Mom, taking a box of eggs from the cupboard.

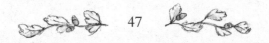

"With syrup?" asked Manu. "Yes, please."

"Blossom's been laying well this week, Jasmine," said Mom, opening the box to reveal six dark-brown speckled eggs.

Blossom was Jasmine's very own hen. On her fifth birthday, Jasmine had opened a wicker basket to find a fluffy yellow day-old chick, nestled in a bed of hay. Blossom had quickly grown into a beautiful hen, and now she lived with the rest

of the chickens, but she was extremely tame and loved to be picked up and cuddled. Jasmine could carry her all around the yard, stroking her silky feathers, while Blossom nestled in her arms, clucking in a low, rhythmic way that sounded almost like purring.

Dad walked into the kitchen in his socks, which had wisps of hay stuck all over them.

"Another nice calf out there," he said. "Lovely little heifer."

A grunt came from the Aga.

Truffle! She was alive! Jasmine felt dizzy with relief.

Mom looked startled. "What was that?"

Jasmine thought quickly. "It was me. Sorry."

"You? What an odd sound to make."

"Sounded like a pig," said Manu.

From the Aga came a little squeal, followed by a scuffling sound.

Everyone stared at the slightly open oven door. Then a change came over Mom's face. Her eyes narrowed and she shifted her gaze to Jasmine, who was sitting on her stool with what she hoped was an innocent, dreamy look on her face.

49

Mom walked over to the Aga. Jasmine sprang up and stood in front of the oven door.

"Jasmine," said Mom, in her quiet-but-deadly voice. "What have you done?"

"Oh, don't be angry," pleaded Jasmine. "I *had* to take her. That horrible farmer was just going to let her die. And she *would* have died, too. She's so tiny you wouldn't believe it. Look. I couldn't have left her, could I?"

And she bent down, reached into the oven, and lifted out the minuscule piglet.

"Oh!" squealed Manu. "That's so cute!"

Mom's face softened as she looked at Truffle. She was trembling a little in Jasmine's arms, but she had her eyes open now, and Jasmine marveled again at their deep-blue color and the length and curl of her lashes.

"My goodness," said Mom. "I think that might be the smallest live pig I've ever seen."

Ella appeared in the doorway in her pajamas. She gasped as her eyes rested on the piglet.

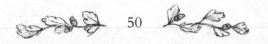

50

"Ohhh!" she squealed. "That is the cutest thing ever. Where did you get it?"

Dad was looking utterly bemused. "Would somebody mind telling me how on earth a piglet has just appeared in our Aga?"

Mom raised her eyebrows at Jasmine. "I think you'd better answer that question, Jas. Don't you?"

7
Running Around the Countryside, Stealing Pigs

"Well, I have to say you've done a great job," said Mom, once Jasmine had explained everything. "That was exactly the right thing to do, giving her colostrum."

"All those hours in the lambing pen paid off, then," said Dad, stroking Truffle's head with a rough, work-hardened finger.

Jasmine was amazed. She needn't have worried after all. All that sneaking around for nothing!

"So where shall we keep her?" she asked.

(Because Mom had checked and Truffle *was* a girl.) "Once she's strong enough, I mean."

Mom stared at her. "Jas," she said gently, "you know you can't keep her. She doesn't belong to you."

"You pignapped her," said Manu.

"But you can't give her back to Mr. Carter," said Ella. "He'll just put her with the other pigs and she'll get crushed."

Jasmine held Truffle tighter. "I'm not taking her back," she said, "and if you try to make me, I'll run away."

Mom sighed. "You can't just take an animal from somebody else's farm. Imagine if someone came up here and took one of Dad's lambs. You wouldn't like that, would you?"

"That's completely different," said Jasmine. "We look after all our lambs. We'd never just leave one to die."

"Even so," said Mom. She turned to Dad. "Come on, Michael, back me up on this."

 53

"Huh?" said Dad, who was tickling Truffle between the ears. Jasmine was delighted to hear Truffle making contented little grunts in response.

"She likes you, Dad," she said.

"I said, can you back me up on this, Michael?" Mom repeated. "We can't have our daughter running around the countryside, stealing pigs."

Dad straightened up. "Well, she'll just have to phone old Carter, won't she?"

"Phone him?" asked Jasmine.

"If you want to keep the pig, that is. Otherwise, just take it back."

Jasmine stared at her father.

"You mean . . . you would let me keep her? But . . . you don't even like pigs."

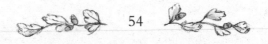

"That's neither here nor there. I doubt he'll let you keep her anyway. He's a miserable old beggar. But you'll never know if you don't ask."

Mom was looking at Dad, shaking her head.

"I don't know. You must be going soft in your old age."

"It won't be forever," said Dad. "Once she's weaned, she'll have to go, like any other farm animal. She's not a pet."

Jasmine opened her mouth to protest, and then thought better of it. She could deal with that later.

Mom was still shaking her head as she found Mr. Carter's number and passed it to Jasmine. Cradling Truffle in one arm, Jasmine picked up the phone. Everyone was silent as she dialed the number. She felt sick.

"Put it on speakerphone," said Ella. "I want to hear this."

The phone rang and rang and Jasmine thought nobody was going to pick up. Then a very grumpy voice grumbled, "Yes?"

Feeling sicker than ever, Jasmine stutteringly explained to Mr. Carter that she had kidnapped his runt. To her amazement, he gave an explosive bark of laughter. Around the table, her family's eyes nearly popped out of their heads.

"I wondered where it was when I looked in this morning," he said. "Thought the sow must have eaten it."

Jasmine shuddered. Mother pigs did sometimes eat their piglets. Imagine if that had happened to Truffle! Thank goodness she had rescued her.

"Still alive, is it?" he asked.

"Yes. She's looking much better."

Immediately she worried she had said the wrong thing. If the farmer thought Truffle was doing well, he might want her back.

"Well, you've done a better job with it than the old sow would have, then."

In a tiny, strained voice, Jasmine said, "Do you . . . do you want her back?"

Mr. Carter gave that barking laugh again. "It

wouldn't last long with that old sow. You'd best hang on to it. What does your dad say?"

Jasmine looked at her dad, who seemed to be listening to the conversation with great interest.

"He says I can keep her until she's weaned."

"Huh. Must be going soft."

Jasmine smiled. "That's exactly what my mom said."

8
She's Smaller Than My Guinea Pigs

When the back doorbell rang an hour later, Jasmine ran to answer it. On the step stood her best friend, Tom, beaming with excitement.

"I can't believe you've got your own piglet," he said, before she even had a chance to say hello. "Where is she?"

He took off his boots and Jasmine led the way into the kitchen, knelt down, and opened the Aga door all the way.

Truffle was still lying on her side, but Jasmine

was delighted to see that her eyes were open and she had stopped shivering.

Tom knelt beside Jasmine. His mouth fell open and his eyes grew very wide.

"She's so tiny! I didn't know pigs could be that small. She's smaller than my guinea pigs."

Jasmine laughed. "That is actually true," she said. Tom's guinea pigs were massive. Probably because Tom fed them two banquets of fresh fruit and vegetables every day, and they had an enormous run in the garden where they could munch on grass the rest of the time.

She lifted Truffle out of the Aga. "Mom just gave her an iron injection," she said.

"Why, is she sick?"

"No, all day-old pigs get one. It keeps them strong. She was very brave. I held her while Mom injected her and she didn't make a sound."

"Can I hold her?" Tom asked.

Jasmine laid Truffle on Tom's knees, and Tom stroked her smooth hair. He looked up at

Jasmine, amazed. "She's so silky and warm."

Truffle raised her head and her little hooves started scrabbling around, as if looking for a foothold.

"Oh, my goodness," said Jasmine. "I think she's trying to stand up."

Gently, she lifted Truffle and stood her on the tiled floor. The piglet wobbled a bit but she stayed upright, looking around curiously.

"She can stand!" said Jasmine. "Mom, come and look!"

Mom came into the kitchen with a basket full of laundry. "Oh, that's a lovely sight. She's definitely better. She won't need to be in the Aga now."

"Shall I put her back in my room?"

"You can for now. Just one more day, though, and then we'll need to find somewhere on the farm for her."

"Oh, but she's too little. Look at her. She'll get cold and lonely outside."

"We'll think of something, and we won't let her get cold or lonely. But she needs to live outside once she's running around, Jasmine. She's going to get pretty messy once she starts eating properly, and she's not house-trained. And no," she said as Jasmine opened her mouth, "you are not going to attempt to house-train her. This house is chaotic enough as it is."

"How did you know what I was going to say?"

Mom raised her eyebrows. "I know how your mind works. Now, I must get this laundry done."

"Should I give her some milk?"

"After you've fed the hens."

Jasmine scooped up the little pig. "Come on, Tom, let's put her in my room while we feed the hens."

"Well done, Jas," said Mom. "You've done a great job with that pig. I think you have a talent for working with animals."

Jasmine glowed. Mom only praised you if she really meant it.

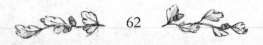

Once they had put Truffle back in her box, Jasmine and Tom pulled on their coats and boots in the mudroom and opened the back door. It was freezing cold this morning, and there was ice on the puddles.

"Poor Bramble," said Tom as they passed the kennel where the old spaniel sat looking out, her big brown eyes mournful. "She looks so sad without Bracken."

"I know," said Jasmine. "She's out on the farm with Dad most of the time, but she must be really lonely when she's in her kennel."

They walked across the yard, smashing the ice on the puddles as they went. It was so much fun to jump onto the smooth ice as hard as you could, hear the satisfying crack, and watch as the muddy brown water beneath oozed through the splits. Jasmine's other favorite thing was to tread really carefully over the ice, hearing it creak and groan under her weight, until it cracked a tiny bit and she could watch the cracks run across the surface of the puddle.

They came to the old cowshed on the other side of the yard, where the hens lived. Jasmine unbolted the top half of the door, opened it, and reached over to unbolt the bottom half. Inside, hens perched on the cobwebbed roof beams and sat in nests they had hollowed out of the deep earth floor.

As Jasmine opened the door, a shaft of morning sunlight spilled into the dim interior. Hens came running out of the shed on their spindly legs, eager for their breakfast. It was a sight that Jasmine never got tired of watching.

And the most eager of all was Blossom, who raced up to Jasmine and started rubbing against her boots.

"Can I feed them?" asked Tom.

Jasmine handed him the basket, which contained a tub of grain, some lettuce leaves, and a few pieces of stale bread. "Crumble the bread into little pieces," she said, "and tear up the lettuce leaves."

While Tom scattered handfuls of grain and crumbled-up crusts around the yard, Jasmine scooped Blossom into her arms. Blossom clucked and cooed as Jasmine stroked her. Her silky feathers were amazing shades of gold and brown, like autumn leaves, with black edges that looked as though they'd been dipped in ink.

"Shall we collect the eggs?" asked Tom when the basket was empty.

"I collect them in the afternoons," said Jasmine. "They generally lay in the mornings."

But Tom looked disappointed, so she said, "But you can go in and see if there are any."

A few minutes later, Tom emerged triumphantly from the darkness with eight smooth, speckled eggs in the basket.

"Tom?" said Jasmine.

"Yes?"

"I've decided what I'm going to do when I'm grown up."

"You're going to have a chicken farm, aren't you?"

"I've changed my mind. I'm going to have an animal rescue center."

Tom's eyes lit up. "Cool! Can I help?"

"You can run it with me. We'll be partners."

"Can we have guinea pigs?"

"We'll have any animal that needs rescuing. Cats, dogs, lambs, piglets . . ."

"Lions, tigers, rhinos . . ."

"Lions and tigers might eat the guinea pigs. And we'd need lots of raw meat to feed them with."

Tom nodded thoughtfully. "Farm animals and pets, then. That will be amazing."

"We'll have to have a farm for them."

"Let's look on the internet. My parents are always looking at houses on the internet."

Jasmine looked at him, alarmed. "Why are they looking at houses? You're not moving away, are you?"

Tom laughed. "No. They're just obsessed with houses."

"OK, let's look for a farm," said Jasmine. "And then we can make plans." She scanned the yard excitedly. "And we should have an office. Where we can write down all our plans and put them

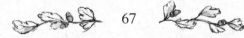

up on the walls. We can find a shed. And you can come up every day over Christmas break to work on the plans."

"I can't. We're going to my granny's," said Tom.

"To Cornwall? For the whole two weeks?"

"Yes. But I'm worried about the guinea pigs. I've never left them for two weeks before. My parents are looking for a boarding place, but what if the people aren't nice?"

Jasmine turned to him with shining eyes. "Let me look after them! I love your guinea pigs and I'd take really good care of them."

Tom's eyes lit up, too. "Oh, would you? That would be amazing. Won't your parents mind?"

"Why would they? I'd be the one doing all the work."

"Let's ask them," said Tom.

"After we've fed Truffle," said Jasmine.

She put Blossom down among the other hens, and they splashed back through the icy puddles. Bramble still looked mournful. Jasmine stroked

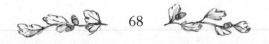

68

her head sadly through the wire of the kennel door. "She needs a friend," she said.

In the mudroom, Jasmine found the big tub of formula milk that Dad kept for the bottle-fed lambs.

"Smell this," she said to Tom. "It's so nice and sweet."

Tom looked suspicious. "Are you tricking me?" He took a quick sniff. "Oh, that *is* nice," he said in surprise. "It smells like cake."

"Mmm," said Jasmine, taking a long sniff. "It reminds me of lambing. I can't wait."

She washed out Truffle's bottle and showed Tom how to make up the formula.

"That's enough shaking," she said finally. "Let's take it to my — oh, no!" She gasped in horror and clapped a hand over her mouth.

"What?" said Tom.

But Jasmine had started to run. "The cats!" she wailed as she raced up the stairs. "I left my bedroom door open! What if they've attacked her?"

 69

Picturing poor, defenseless little Truffle covered in bites and scratches, Jasmine burst through her bedroom door and darted around the end of the bed.

"Oh!" she exclaimed.

"What's happened?" asked Tom, running into the room. "Is she OK?"

"Oh, Tom," said Jasmine. "Look at this."

Tom looked. "Oh!" he said. "That's amazing."

Jasmine ran to her bedroom door. "Mom!" she called. "Come and look at this."

Mom emerged from her office, holding the phone in one hand and a letter in the other. "Is it important? I'm working."

"It's very important. It won't take long, but there's something you need to see."

She took Mom's arm and pulled her over to where Tom was kneeling beside Truffle's box.

"Oh, my," said Mom. "That is so sweet."

The tiny pig lay asleep in the straw, breathing quietly and steadily. Curled around her, each

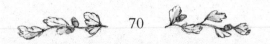

twice her size and both fast asleep, too, were Toffee and Marmite. It was the most peaceful sight you could possibly imagine.

"Have you ever seen that before?" asked Jasmine. "Piglets and cats being friends?"

Mom shook her head, smiling. "Never," she said. "That is really very special."

Jasmine looked pleadingly at her mother.

"So you can't turn her outside now, can you? She's very special, you just said so."

Mom laughed. "Nice try, Jasmine. You have to remember she's a pig, not a cat or a dog. You saw the size of her mother. I know she's tiny now, but she'll grow very quickly. She's not an indoor animal."

Suddenly, Jasmine had a thought. It was so obvious she couldn't believe she hadn't thought of it before.

She looked up at Mom, her eyes full of excitement.

"Maybe she can't live inside forever," she said, "but I know someone she could live with outside. Someone who really needs a friend right now."

9
I've Got a New Idea

The sun came out for the first day of Christmas break. The frost that coated every blade of grass sparkled like diamonds as Jasmine opened the gate into the orchard, a bottle of warm milk in her hand.

She opened her mouth to call Truffle, but the sturdy little piglet was already galloping across the frosty grass on her tiny hooves, squealing with excitement. Beside her, tail wagging wildly, bounded Bramble. She looked like a completely different dog from the one who had sat mournfully alone in her kennel a month ago.

Truffle clamped the teat in her mouth and started to guzzle the milk, her curly tail wriggling with pleasure. Jasmine thought back to her first desperate attempts to get her to swallow. These days, she had to grip the bottle hard or Truffle would pull it out of her hands with the force of her sucking. It took less than a minute for her to guzzle the whole thing.

"That's it, Truffle, sorry," said Jasmine. The piglet was still sucking on thin air, and Jasmine had to wrestle the empty bottle away from her. She took a threadbare tennis ball from her pocket.

"Look! Playtime!"

Truffle squealed with excitement. Jasmine hurled the ball as far as she could, and the piglet bounded across the grass between the fruit trees in pursuit. Bramble looked on proudly as Truffle raced back with the tennis ball clamped between her jaws.

"Good girl," said Jasmine, scratching Truffle's soft belly. The pig flopped onto her side, grunting with pleasure.

Dad and Manu were walking toward the orchard from the field. "Bramble!" called Dad.

He opened the gate from the orchard into the farmyard, and Bramble ran out to greet him. She might be old, but there was still nothing she liked more than a walk around the fields with her master.

Dad frowned as he looked over the fence at the grass. "That pig's made a mess of the orchard, rooting around."

"It's not her fault," Jasmine said. "It's her instincts. She can smell things up to six feet underground. Did you know that? That's why they use pigs to sniff out truffles in Italy."

Manu broke into peals of laughter. "Truffles! Why do they bury chocolates underground?"

"Not that sort of truffle," said Jasmine. "They're a kind of underground fungus."

76

"Oh," said Manu, understanding dawning on his face. "Is that why you called her Truffle?"

"Well, there are no truffles here," said Dad, "and she's ruining the grass. Come on, Bramble. Let's go and check those sheep."

Jasmine heard a car engine. "Ooh, Truffle," she said, "that must be Tom with the guinea pigs! I'm going to go settle them in, and then we'll come and play with you."

In the yard, Tom's mom, Miss Mel, switched off the car engine. Tom got out of the back seat slowly, holding a plastic carrying case with a wire grid at the front. His usually cheerful face looked tense and anxious.

"They hate traveling," he said. "They've burrowed into the hay and they're frozen with fright."

"Oh, poor things," said Jasmine. She bent down and peered through the wire, but she couldn't even see Snowy and Twiglet in the mound of hay.

"They'll be fine once they're in a hutch again,"

said Miss Mel. "Hello, Jasmine, how are you? I hear you're bringing up a pig."

"Yes," said Jasmine. "Her name is Truffle."

"She's the best pig in the world," said Tom. Then he spoke softly into the carrying case. "And you're the best guinea pigs in the world, aren't you?" He turned to Jasmine. "I don't want to offend them."

"Come and see their hutch," said Jasmine.

"Before you go, Jasmine," said Miss Mel, "we wanted to give you this." She held out an envelope.

"Oh, thank you," said Jasmine, curious.

"Open it," said Tom. He looked excited.

Jasmine opened the envelope. She stared in amazement. Inside were several bills.

"Money?" she said. "For looking after the guinea pigs? Oh, no, you don't have to pay me. Honestly, I want to look after them."

She held out the envelope to Miss Mel, but Miss Mel smiled and shook her head. "I know you're not doing it for money," she said, "but if we boarded them, we'd have to pay, and we know

you'll look after them better than any boarding place would. Tom's told us all about how you nursed Truffle back to life."

Jasmine was almost speechless. "Thank you," she said. "Thank you so much."

"Thank *you*," said Miss Mel. "Tom adores his guinea pigs, and we're very grateful to you for having them. Now, I'm just going to pop into the house and say hello to your mom."

Jasmine's mind was racing as she led the way through the gate and down the walkway. Money! Money of her own! Lots of money! And for looking after two adorable guinea pigs!

By the time she had reached the lawn, her plan was formed.

"I've got a new idea," she said to Tom. "About what I'm going to do when I grow up."

"You don't want to have the rescue center anymore?"

"Oh, yes, I definitely do. But Mom and Dad said it will cost a lot of money, because you have to get the land and then feed all the animals. But now that's OK because I'm going to board animals there, too, you see. So people will pay for me to look after their pets while they're on vacation, and that money will pay to look after the rescued animals."

Tom looked impressed. "That's a great idea."

"And your guinea pigs will be the first animals boarded with me. I hope they like it here."

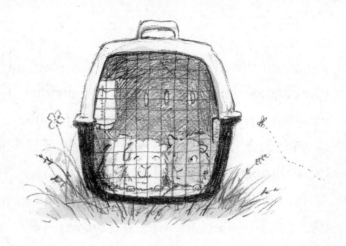

10
A Fully Trained Sniffer Pig

"I've scrubbed out the coop that Blossom lived in when she was a chick," Jasmine said, leading Tom across the garden. "It's got a big run with it, too, see."

"It's lovely," said Tom. "Bigger than their hutch at home. Look, guineas, this is your vacation house. And Jasmine's put some food in it for you, too. Carrots and curly kale, your favorites."

He set the case down gently on the grass and unclipped the front. From the heap of hay came scuffling and rustling sounds.

Jasmine lifted up the hinged wooden lid of the chicken coop. The inside was divided by a wooden partition into two rooms. Jasmine had covered the floor with wood shavings and filled the bedroom with fresh hay.

Tom reached into the case and lifted out a bundle of snow-white fur with big brown eyes.

"Hello, Snowy," said Jasmine, taking him from Tom. "Oh, you're so soft."

She could feel Snowy's racing heartbeat under his thick, soft fur. She stroked him gently. "Don't worry," she murmured. "You're going to be all right. You'll have a lovely time here."

Tom took Snowy's brother, Twiglet, from the

case. He was reddish with black eyes. "Shall we put them in the hutch?" he said. "They probably need to get used to it."

Gently, they lowered the guinea pigs into the hutch, next to the food bowl. They stood there, frozen to the spot. Jasmine picked up a piece of carrot and held it out. They stayed frozen. Slowly, she moved the carrot right in front of Twiglet's nose.

Twiglet made a tiny movement and grabbed the end of the carrot. He scurried into the bedroom, the carrot clamped in his mouth. Then he dropped it on the shavings and began to nibble frantically.

"Oh, that's good," said Tom. "If he's eating, he must be happy."

Suddenly, Snowy unfroze and scuttled after his brother. He snatched up the piece of carrot from under Twiglet's nose and disappeared into the pile of hay.

Jasmine laughed. "Poor Twiglet! That's so mean!"

"They're always doing that to each other," said Tom. "Whichever one gets a piece of food first, the other one snatches it. But they don't seem to mind. The first one just goes and gets another piece. I think it's a game. You just have to make sure you always give them two of everything."

Sure enough, Twiglet approached the food again, snuffled around, and found another piece of carrot. He grabbed it and ran back to the bedroom.

"I'm glad you've got two of them," said Jasmine. "It must be very lonely for them if there's only one."

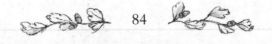

"In Switzerland, it's illegal to keep only one," said Tom.

"Is it really?"

"It's because they're social animals. They say it's cruel to keep one on its own. Same with rabbits."

"That's a good law," said Jasmine. "I like Switzerland."

"Twiglet and Snowy definitely like being together," said Tom. "They sleep next to each other, and they always go out in their run together. And they wrestle, too."

"Wrestle?"

"Yes, it's so funny. They run around and one of them jumps on top of the other and they wrestle. They don't hurt each other. It's just play-fighting. I gave them a ball, too, but they never play with it."

The guinea pigs had burrowed into the hay and were invisible now. Munching and crunching sounds came from the hay. Tom gently lowered the hinged lid of the hutch.

"Let's play fetch with Truffle," said Jasmine. She took the battered tennis ball from her pocket.

Tom looked at it.

"Would Truffle like the guinea pigs' ball?" he asked.

"Really? Are you sure?"

"Like I said, they never play with it. I think it's too big for them. I'll get them a Ping-Pong ball instead."

"OK, then. Thanks. Truffle's wrecked this one already."

"Has your dad changed his mind yet?" asked Tom as they walked to the orchard. "About you keeping Truffle?"

"No," said Jasmine gloomily. "He just says she might be cute now but what happens when she's fully grown? He says he's not a pig farmer and he can't keep a full-size pig around doing nothing and ruining the grass and costing a fortune to feed."

"Shh," said Tom. "She'll hear you."

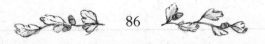

Truffle was running across the orchard to greet them. Tom held out the ball. "Here, Truffle. A present for you."

Truffle sniffed at the ball. Tom dropped it on the ground. Truffle nuzzled it with her snout, grunting and snuffling. She nudged it and rolled it over, smelling every millimeter of its surface.

"Aren't pigs' snouts amazing?" said Jasmine. "They have millions of scent receptors, even more than dogs. And their snouts are really hard under the skin, so they can use them for digging and moving things around as well as smelling stuff."

"She's really sniffing that," said Tom. "She must be able to smell the guinea pigs on it."

"She definitely can," said Jasmine. Then she drew in her breath. "I know! I'm going to train Truffle as a sniffer pig!"

"A sniffer pig?"

"They do exist. I've read about it. They can be trained just like the sniffer dogs the police use to track down criminals and things."

"But how do you train them?"

"I've watched lots of stuff about training sniffer dogs," said Jasmine. "You start by just playing with

the object you want her to find. We'll play fetch with that ball, like we do already."

Tom picked up the ball and laughed. "Ugh, it's covered in slobber."

He lifted the ball behind his head. Truffle was instantly alert, her body still, her eyes focused on the ball in Tom's hand.

"Fetch!" called Tom, throwing the ball across the orchard. Truffle bounded across the grass and raced back to the children, the ball in her mouth, her tail wriggling excitedly.

"Good girl," said Tom, reaching out to pat her.

"Wait," said Jasmine. "Sit, Truffle."

Truffle stood looking at her.

"Truffle, sit."

Jasmine put her hand on Truffle's back. Truffle sat, looking up at her expectantly.

"Good pig," said Jasmine, crouching down and scratching her between the ears. "Good pig."

Tom looked from Truffle to Jasmine, wide-eyed. "Wow. How did you train her to sit?"

"Same as a dog," said Jasmine. "Pigs are just as clever as dogs, so there's no reason why you can't train them in the same way."

After they had played a few more games of fetch, Jasmine said, "Now she's ready for the next stage. That's where we teach her to play hide-and-seek, only by using smell instead of sight. It's what pigs do naturally. We're just training her to do it with this object. Come, Truffle."

Truffle trotted along with them to a pile of dead leaves in the corner of the orchard.

"First, we let her see us hide the ball," said Jasmine. "Here, Truffle."

She held out the ball. Truffle made as if to grab it, but Jasmine buried the ball in the leaves.

"Find it!" she said. She turned to Tom. "That's the command we're teaching her. Every time we say, 'Find it!' she has to search for the ball. Then we reward her."

"With food?"

"No, with praise and play. That's the best way to reward sniffer dogs—or sniffer pigs. It's what they like most."

Truffle was snuffling in the leaves, shifting the pile around with her snout. Now she uncovered the ball and picked it up.

"Good pig!" said Jasmine. "Good pig!" She took the ball and scratched Truffle along her belly. The little piglet flopped over, grunting with pleasure.

Tom laughed. "It's amazing, all her different grunts and squeals. It's like she's really talking."

"Of course she's talking," said Jasmine. "Good pig, Truffle. Now watch this."

She hid the ball under the leaves again and gave the command. "Find it!"

Truffle found it quickly this time, pulling it out of the heap and shaking off the dry, brown leaves that had stuck to her face.

"She's a quick learner," said Tom as he scratched the pig's belly.

"Yes, it won't take long to train her."

"So what's the next stage?"

"One of us holds her and the other one hides the ball without her seeing, so she has to find it using only her sense of smell. We hide it somewhere close at first, and then gradually make it harder. You'll see. By the time you come back from Cornwall, I'll have a fully trained sniffer pig. The police will be begging me for her."

11
If She's Chasing the Chickens . . .

Mom was handing plates of pasta to Jasmine and Tom for lunch when her phone rang. She went into the hall to answer it. When she returned, she said, "I've got to go and see a horse at Turner's. Will you two be all right? Ella's upstairs if you need her. Daddy's out with the calves. OK?"

"We'll be fine," Jasmine assured her.

"Ella's the best babysitter," said Tom as Jasmine's mom drove out of the yard. "She wouldn't notice if we burned the house down."

"No, she'd probably just look up from her books as the flames were licking the edge of her desk," said Jasmine, "and think it was getting nice and warm in her room."

"And then—"

Jasmine grabbed his arm. "Shhh. What was that?"

Piercing squeals and shrieks were coming from somewhere outside. Tom and Jasmine looked at each other in alarm.

"It's Truffle," said Jasmine, jumping up from the table. "Something bad's happening. She's never squealed like that before."

They ran into the mudroom and shoved their feet into their boots. In the middle of tugging on her left one, Jasmine froze.

Truffle's shrieking had drowned out every other sound. But now Jasmine heard something else. The panicked squawking of the hens.

"Oh, no!" she gasped. "If she's chasing the chickens . . ."

She didn't dare finish that sentence. If Truffle

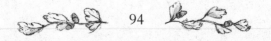

94

had escaped from the orchard and was chasing the chickens, Dad would send her to market without a second thought, and nothing Jasmine could say would change his mind.

She raced outside. A glance over the orchard fence showed her that Truffle had not escaped into the yard. She was still in the orchard, squealing up a storm, her front hooves planted against the fence.

Something was very wrong.

In the yard, the chickens were running around in panicked circles, flapping their wings and squawking, some of them flapping up into the low branches of the trees.

Was it Truffle's shrieks that had made them panic? Or was Truffle warning the hens?

Jasmine tugged back the bolt on the garden gate, and she and Tom raced into the yard, making the hens panic even more.

"Look!" yelled Jasmine, pointing to the corner of the cowshed.

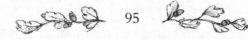

Slinking off around the side of the building was a huge fox. And in its mouth was a hen.

The hen hung limply from the fox's jaws. Jasmine couldn't tell if she was alive or dead. Foxes often snatched their prey alive and killed it later.

"NO!" she yelled. "Put that down, you horrible creature!"

If she could get the fox to drop the hen, she might be in time to save her. She raced after it, slowing only to pick up a rusty old piece of pipe by the cowshed wall. She flung the pipe at the animal. To her surprise and satisfaction, it struck the fox's backside. The fox yelped and sped up with Jasmine chasing it, still shouting.

The fox was outstripping her easily now, but Jasmine knew it couldn't keep up that pace with a chicken dangling from its mouth.

Sure enough, after a few more seconds, it dropped the hen, increased its stride, and was gone through the hedge and up into the next field.

Jasmine tore across the bumpy ground, stumbling in the ruts, the clay soil sticking to her boots, until she reached the bundle of feathers dumped on the wet grass.

Sometimes a chicken taken in this way was merely stunned. Sometimes it would get up and walk away, dazed but unharmed. But Jasmine knew, from the way this one was lying, that she was dead.

It wasn't until she bent down over the body, though, that she recognized the hen.

It was Blossom.

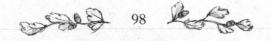

12
That Wind's Getting Up

Everyone told Jasmine that Blossom had had a good life, that she had been very lucky to be loved so much, and that her death was quick and painless. But none of that consoled Jasmine in the slightest. Blossom would have lived for many more years, she was sure, if that horrible fox hadn't killed her. And of *course* she had suffered.

Whenever Jasmine thought of the terror poor Blossom must have felt when that fox sank its snarling teeth into her and carried her off across

the field, she started sobbing all over again.

Her only comfort was her animals. She spent hours every day cuddling the guinea pigs and training Truffle. And Truffle was a very quick learner. After a week of daily training, Jasmine could shut her in the kennel while she hid the guinea pigs' tennis ball anywhere in the orchard. Then she would let Truffle out and on the command "Find it!" she could sniff out the ball wherever Jasmine had hidden it.

She took her for walks across the field and up the farm road, too, with Bracken's old collar and

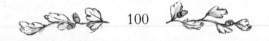

leash. Truffle trotted along with her just like an obedient dog, and she was a very good listener. One day, they walked up to the woods behind the farm and cut sprigs of holly to decorate the living room.

"Aren't they beautiful, Truffle," said Jasmine as she arranged holly sprigs in a jam jar to put on Blossom's grave, "with those shiny dark leaves and scarlet berries?"

"What would you like for Christmas?" Mom and Dad kept asking her. And Jasmine always gave the same answer.

"I want to keep Truffle."

Her parents would raise their eyebrows, and Mom would take a deep breath and say, "I know you do, Jasmine. But since that isn't possible, what else would you like?"

To keep her parents happy, Jasmine suggested a few little things. But really, the only thing she wanted was to keep her pig.

As it drew closer and closer to Christmas,

though, Jasmine couldn't help getting excited. She helped Mom bake mince pies and she helped Dad decorate the hall and living room, and the house started to feel very Christmassy indeed.

And finally it was Christmas Eve, and time to do the one thing they always saved for last. Right after breakfast, Jasmine, Manu, and even Ella climbed into the open back of Dad's pickup truck and bumped across the fields to the little Christmas tree area next to the woods.

Several years ago, Dad had experimented with growing Christmas trees to sell. The soil hadn't been right, and the experiment wasn't a success, but a few trees had survived.

They weren't as perfect as you would find on a tree farm. A bit of clever decorating was always needed to cover the bald patches and the weird

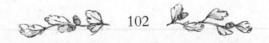

parts. But once they had covered it with tinsel and ornaments and lights, Jasmine always thought their tree looked magical.

The tree they chose this year was the biggest one so far. Mom wouldn't know what to do.

"Not too big," she said every year, "or we won't all fit in the room."

But they never paid any attention. With Christmas trees, the rest of them all agreed, bigger was definitely better.

They held the tree steady while Dad sawed through the trunk. The wind was bitingly cold and Jasmine was glad she had worn her gloves. When the tree was cut, they all piled into the back of the truck. Dad lifted the tree onto their knees. It prickled their faces as they jolted over the rutted ground, singing "Jingle Bells" and

"Sleigh Ride." At that moment, Jasmine felt properly Christmassy.

"That wind's getting up," said Dad as he heaved the enormous tree out of the truck. "Shouldn't be surprised if it snows later. This is some tree. Mom's in for a shock."

Snow! Jasmine loved snow, but she did worry about the guinea pigs. What if they froze to death?

"Give them extra hay so they can burrow right into it," Mom said when Jasmine asked her advice later that afternoon. She had finally stopped ranting about the size of the tree, so it was safe to speak to her again.

"I've already given them lots of extra hay. And I put an old blanket over the hutch."

"Then you've done the right thing. They'll be fine. They've got all that fur, remember. Now where did I put my car keys? I'll be back in a couple of hours, in time to decorate the tree and hang up the stockings."

Mom was taking Manu and Ben to a Christmas

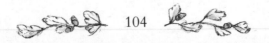

Eve party at a friend's house. Dad was feeding the calves. Ella was upstairs. It was only four thirty, but it was already dark. Too dark to play with Truffle, who was snuggled up in the kennel with Bramble, warm and cozy and full of milk.

Mom opened the front door and a gust of freezing wind blew in. "Oh, it's horrible out there. Boys, are you coming?"

Jasmine went to look at the Christmas tree. It was beautiful, but the house felt too quiet and empty. The wind whipped strands of ivy against the windows. Jasmine closed the curtains. She wished there was a fire, but she wasn't allowed to light it when there was no adult around. She went up to her room and took out her drawing paper and pencils.

She became so absorbed in drawing a picture of a field full of pigs that she tuned out the outside world completely. It was only when she finished it and realized she was hungry that she noticed the wind was much fiercer now. It howled in the chimneys and rattled the doors.

It was time to give the guinea pigs their evening feed. She put some carrots and cabbage leaves in a bowl and pulled on her coat and boots in the mudroom. An icy wind blew under the back door, rattling at the catch. When Jasmine opened the door, the cabbage leaves flew out of the bowl and she was almost blown back into the

106

room. She scrabbled on the floor to pick up the leaves and clamped a hand over the bowl as she went out. The wind was blowing the door inward and she couldn't shut it with one hand, so she had to stuff the food into her pocket and abandon the bowl. She put her flashlight in the other pocket and grabbed the door handle with both hands to play tug-of-war with the gale.

Once she had finally yanked the door shut, she made her way along the walkway, head down, one hand in her pocket and the other holding her flashlight. The wind was behind her now and its force propelled her down the path. She had never felt wind like it.

She came to the end of the path and stepped onto the lawn. Then she gasped in horror.

The guinea pigs' hutch had blown right over. It was lying on its back on the grass. And the roof was completely open.

"Oh, no! Oh, no!" cried Jasmine. She ran to the fallen hutch and shone her flashlight inside.

The guinea pigs weren't there.

13
We've Got Work to Do

Jasmine desperately shone her flashlight into every corner of the empty hutch. Terrible pictures flashed into her mind. Were the guinea pigs crushed under the hutch? Had the fox taken them? Had the cats gotten them? Were they freezing to death in a hedge? Or had they run so far away that she would never find them again?

How could she ever tell Tom? He had trusted her with his precious pets, and look what she had done. She wasn't worthy to look after

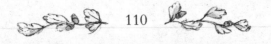

animals. This would never have happened if Tom had boarded them.

All this went through Jasmine's mind in a couple of seconds. And then she came to her senses.

Stop panicking, she told herself, *and find the guinea pigs. That's the only thing that matters.*

The first thing to do was to lift the hutch up. The thought of what she might find underneath was unbearable, but she had to do it.

She pulled the lid shut, crouched down, and slid her fingers under the edges of the fallen hutch. She took a firm grip. Then, with all her strength, she pushed it upright. Feeling sick, she made herself shine her flashlight on the ground where the hutch had fallen.

Relief swept over her. The guinea pigs weren't crushed.

But the relief only lasted a second. Because if

they weren't under the hutch, then where were they?

Jasmine straightened up and swept her flashlight around the garden. Panic overwhelmed her. It was a big garden, with a lot of shrubs in the flower border and on the lawn. And it was enclosed on two sides by a dense, prickly hawthorn hedge. How long would it take to search all that? And what might happen to the poor little guinea pigs in the meantime?

At least Snowy would show up easily with the flashlight. Unless it started to snow, of course.

Oh, please don't let it snow, Jasmine thought. *Not now. Not while Snowy and Twiglet are out in the wild.*

She lay on the freezing lawn in front of the nearest bush. She parted the twigs and swept the flashlight beam over the ground.

"Snowy! Twiglet!" she called softly. "Come on, boys. Come on, babies."

No, unless they were hiding very well indeed,

they weren't in that bush. She scanned the lawn with her flashlight again. No sign of them on the grass. She searched the other shrubs, first checking the ones nearest the hutch and then gradually moving farther away, calling softly the whole time.

By the time she had searched every bush in the garden, Jasmine's hands were numb and her feet felt like blocks of ice in her boots. Her teeth chattered and her head throbbed. But she had to go on. Giving up was unthinkable.

She looked at the hedge with a feeling of

dread. She and Tom had once spent a morning building a den in there. After two hours of tunneling through hawthorn, they were covered in scratches that stung for days.

But now she had no choice.

She would burrow into the hedge and crawl right through it, the whole way around the garden. It was hollow inside, so once she was in, it shouldn't be too bad. *Oh, please,* she thought, *please let the guinea pigs be sheltering in there.*

Because if they weren't in the garden, then what would she do? They could have run in any direction. What possible hope did she have of finding them?

If they hadn't been caught already.

She mustn't think about that. She would start here, by the orchard fence.

The orchard fence . . .

Jasmine's eyes widened.

The orchard!

Truffle!

113

How could she have been so careless? Crawling under bushes, wasting goodness knows how much time, when she had a fully trained sniffer pig sitting in the kennel.

She battled up the walkway, her eyes streaming from the biting wind. Her mind was whirling. Truffle was used to sniffing out her ball, and the scent on her ball was the scent of the guinea pigs, so surely it should work.

But would it?

Jasmine reached the front garden. She took Truffle's collar and leash off the hook by the kennel door.

"Truffle!" she called. "Come here, Truffle."

Truffle didn't need to be called twice. Before Jasmine had finished saying the words, the piglet was at the kennel door, squealing in anticipation. Jasmine shone her flashlight inside. Bramble looked up sleepily from her basket. Jasmine unbolted the door and opened it just wide enough for Truffle to get out. She bolted it shut again and slipped the

114

collar over Truffle's head. She stroked her smooth, sleek back and silky ears. Her skin was so warm. Jasmine felt bad about bringing her out into the freezing night, but she didn't seem to mind.

"Come on, Truffle," said Jasmine, leading her pig down the walkway. "We've got work to do."

14
Find It, Truffle!

Outside the guinea pigs' hutch, Jasmine crouched down next to Truffle.

"Find it, Truffle," she said. "Find it!"

Truffle was already sniffing the ground, her snout quivering just above the grass. She seemed excited. She must recognize the scent of her ball, Jasmine thought.

"Find it!" she said again, encouragingly.

Truffle kept sniffing.

"Find it!" Jasmine said, trying to sound relaxed

and positive. Inside, though, she felt desperate. Truffle was her only hope. She would never find Twiglet and Snowy on her own.

Truffle continued to sniff around the hutch. And in the glow of her flashlight, Jasmine saw white flakes falling.

Snow!

Jasmine had been wishing for a white Christmas for years. But right now, it was the last thing she wanted. It was bad enough that the guinea pigs were out in this bitter wind, without snow to make them even colder.

"Find it!" she said urgently. "Find it!"

And Truffle started edging away from the hutch, her snout still quivering just above the ground. Jasmine's heart sped up. Could she really have picked up a trail?

Holding tightly to the end of the leash, Jasmine crept behind Truffle as she sniffed her way across the garden. She hardly dared breathe. She mustn't distract her. It would be best if Truffle didn't

even realize Jasmine was there. She wasn't used to being on a leash while she searched. But Jasmine didn't dare let her off the leash tonight. Because it wouldn't be a ball she found at the end of the trail, would it? It would be two very frightened guinea pigs. And it wouldn't do them any good at all to be grabbed in a pig's jaws like a tennis ball.

Truffle made her way straight to the hedge. Jasmine's heart sank. Now she was going to have to crawl through it. But of course the guinea pigs would go to the hedge. They would naturally choose the safest route.

Truffle was straining at the leash, snuffling at the ground. Jasmine got down on her hands and knees, bunched up the leash in her hand, and wriggled after her into the hedge. Twigs snapped and thorns scratched her face as she wormed her way into the hollow center. She screwed up her face in pain as she knelt on a sharp stone, but she managed not to make a sound. She mustn't do anything to put Truffle off the scent.

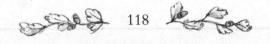

118

Truffle snuffled her way enthusiastically right along the middle of the hedge. How far had the guinea pigs gone? Were they still in here? If they were, at least they might be safe. Although a hedge wouldn't be a barrier to a hungry fox.

She mustn't think about that. She just hoped Truffle *was* actually on the trail of the guinea pigs. What if she was following a completely different scent? What if she wasn't following any scent at all, but just going for a stroll along the middle of a hedgerow?

They had reached the far corner of the garden. Truffle turned right, following the hedge along the bottom of the orchard. Jasmine got something in her eye when a twig snapped against the side of her face, but she couldn't stop. She just kept blinking and hoping it would get dislodged. Her face was smarting with the scratches and her knees throbbed from crawling over roots and stones. Her hair kept getting caught in thorns and she just had to yank it free. The only good thing was that at least

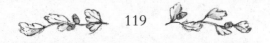

119

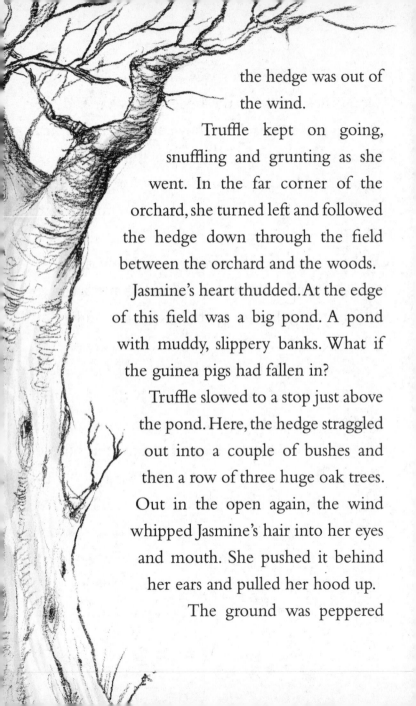

the hedge was out of the wind.

Truffle kept on going, snuffling and grunting as she went. In the far corner of the orchard, she turned left and followed the hedge down through the field between the orchard and the woods.

Jasmine's heart thudded. At the edge of this field was a big pond. A pond with muddy, slippery banks. What if the guinea pigs had fallen in?

Truffle slowed to a stop just above the pond. Here, the hedge straggled out into a couple of bushes and then a row of three huge oak trees. Out in the open again, the wind whipped Jasmine's hair into her eyes and mouth. She pushed it behind her ears and pulled her hood up.

The ground was peppered

with rabbit holes. Jasmine's flashlight picked out a pair of startled rabbit eyes. The rabbit froze for a couple of seconds before it bolted away.

Truffle was nuzzling around the burrows. Had she gotten distracted by the smell of rabbit and lost the guinea pig scent?

"Find it!" Jasmine urged. "Find it, Truffle!"

Truffle seemed particularly interested in one big rabbit hole near the hedge.

"Not rabbits," said Jasmine. "Guinea pigs! It's guinea pigs we need, Truffle. Go on. Find it!"

But Truffle kept snuffling at the rabbit hole.

She was getting frantic now, grunting excitedly, shoving her snout right in the opening and digging out the soil.

Jasmine frowned. This wasn't typical Truffle behavior. She had never been interested in rabbit holes before.

Could the guinea pigs have chosen this burrow as their hiding place?

"Good girl, Truffle," she said. "Now sit. *Sit*."

She pressed her hand down firmly on the piglet's back end. Reluctantly, Truffle stopped digging and sat, her snout still quivering.

"Good girl," said Jasmine, scratching her between the ears. "Good girl."

She shone her flashlight around until she spotted a sturdy-looking low branch in the hedge. She noticed with alarm that the flashlight beam was getting fainter. The battery must be running low.

She tied Truffle's leash firmly to the branch. "Sit there, Truffle."

Feeling sick with nerves, Jasmine shone the

fading light into the rabbit hole. And there, far, far down, huddled two bundles of quivering fur, staring out at her, frozen in terror.

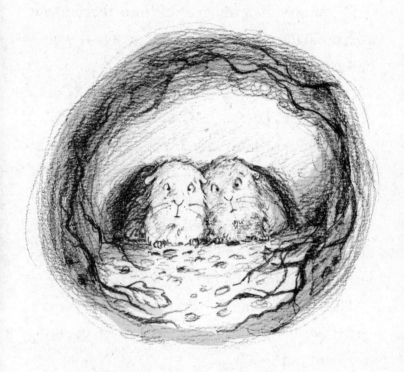

"Oh!" breathed Jasmine, letting out her pent-up breath in a huge sigh of relief. "Oh, there you are! You're alive! We've found you! You're safe!"

She turned to Truffle and gave her an enormous

hug. "You did it, Truffle! You found the guinea pigs! You clever, clever girl. Now we just have to get them out of that hole."

She shone the fading beam into the burrow, glad the light was weak now. Hopefully it would be less scary for the guinea pigs.

"Come on, Snowy," she coaxed softly. "Come on, Twiglet. Come on, boys, you're all safe now."

The guinea pigs didn't move. Very slowly, Jasmine extended her right arm into the burrow. If they stayed frozen, she could lift them out.

But as her arm moved closer to them, the guinea pigs squeaked in alarm and scuttled backward, farther into the burrow.

That wasn't going to work, then. Jasmine slowly withdrew her arm. How was she ever going to get them out?

Then she remembered. She had carrots and cabbage in her pockets.

She took out a long piece of carrot. Guinea pigs were supposed to have an excellent sense of

smell. And these two were probably hungry by now. If she could just tempt them out . . .

She held the carrot out toward them. The guinea pigs gave frightened squeaks and shuffled back again. Jasmine dropped the carrot on the floor of the burrow, withdrew her hand, and waited. She tried not to think about how cold she was.

"We might be waiting a long time, Truffle," she said. "But that's OK. You deserve a very good scratch for all your hard work. And a treat."

She fed Truffle half a carrot, which the piglet crunched up in her mouth, grunting happily. Then Jasmine scratched her belly until she flopped over onto her side with sheer pleasure.

Still scratching Truffle with one hand, Jasmine leaned over and peered into the burrow, shining the flashlight to one side of the hole so as not to startle the guinea pigs.

"Oh," she said, in the tiniest whisper. "It's working."

Twiglet was approaching the carrot. Just as he

clamped it in his mouth, Jasmine reached out, grabbed him around the middle, and lifted him out of the hole. Twiglet squealed, but when Jasmine held him close and stroked him, he quieted. His heart was beating so fast that Jasmine feared it would burst.

Now for Snowy. Holding Twiglet's warm body against her coat, Jasmine gently placed another piece of carrot near the mouth of the burrow.

Snowy was more timid than his brother, and Jasmine sat shivering on the freezing ground for a long time, talking in a soft voice that she hoped would soothe both Twiglet in her arms and Snowy in the burrow. It must have soothed Truffle, anyway, because she sat quietly, only giving an occasional contented low grunt.

Eventually, Jasmine heard the sound she had been waiting for. A tiny scrabbling noise, followed by a frantic crunching of carrot.

Holding her breath and moving as stealthily as she could, Jasmine stretched her arm into the

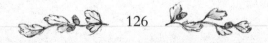

burrow and grasped Snowy around the middle. He squealed and wriggled, but Jasmine kept hold of him and lifted him out.

Two guinea pigs, safe in her arms! Jasmine had never been so relieved in her life. She stroked and soothed them until they had calmed a little. Their warm bodies felt like hot water bottles for her freezing hands. Thank goodness they had such thick fur.

Once the guinea pigs were calm, Jasmine tried to untie Truffle's leash from the branch. This proved impossible with a guinea pig in each arm, so she just unclipped the leash from the collar. She would have to come back and fetch it tomorrow.

Tomorrow! Jasmine suddenly remembered that tomorrow was Christmas Day. Everything was all right again. Snowy and Twiglet were safe and sound, and her pig had found them.

"Come on, Truffle," she said. "Home time."

As they walked back to the house, the snow started to fall thickly and steadily. Jasmine kept her eyes on the ground. She didn't want to stumble into a rabbit hole with the guinea pigs in her arms. Her flashlight beam was now just a feeble pinprick of light.

Halfway across the field, she thought she heard shouting. She looked up. Several flashlight beams swept across the garden, the farmyard, the next field, and now the field she was in. What was going on?

She stopped and listened. What were they shouting?

They were calling her name! Why were they calling her name?

Suddenly she was lit up in a beam of light.

"Jasmine!" shouted Mom. "Oh, Jasmine, where have you been?"

Mom started running across the field. "She's here! Jasmine's here!"

And now Mom reached her and flung her arms around her. "Oh, Jas, where have you been? We've been completely frantic."

"Don't squash the guinea pigs," Jasmine tried to say, but her teeth were chattering so much and her lips were so numb that she couldn't speak.

Her mom released her. "Are you all right? What happened?"

She shone her flashlight into Jasmine's face. Jasmine flinched and screwed her eyes shut.

Mom gasped. "Your lips are purple. And you're covered in scratches." She touched Jasmine's cheek. "Oh, you're like a block of ice. What on earth happened to you?"

"I'm fine," Jasmine managed to say through her chattering teeth. "I was on a rescue mission."

15
Jasmine First

The first thing Jasmine saw when she woke up the next morning was the bulging stocking at the end of her bed, with a chocolate Father Christmas peeping out the top. She smiled to herself. It was really Christmas Day. And all her animals were safe.

She swung her legs out of bed and hurried to the window. Dad had promised he would put heavy weights on the hutch roof to make sure it wouldn't blow over again, but she had to make sure everything was all right.

She pulled the curtains open and gasped. Outside was a fairy-tale world. The ground was covered in a dazzling white carpet of snow. Every twig on every tree was coated with snow. And the guinea pigs' hutch was safe and sound under a snow blanket.

It wasn't until four in the afternoon, when the animals had all been fed and checked and

Mom had returned from an emergency foaling, that the family sat down in front of a roaring log fire to admire the Christmas tree and open their presents.

"Jasmine first!" said Manu, who was bouncing up and down with excitement.

Ella handed Jasmine a present. Jasmine could tell immediately that it was a book, although she could have guessed that before she saw it. Ella always gave books.

It was called *The Porcine Encyclopedia: All You Need to Know About the Care and Treatment of Pigs.* Jasmine was touched by Ella's thoughtfulness, and tried not to think about Truffle being sold in a few months' time.

Manu needed Dad's help to lift his enormous present from under the tree and carry it over to Jasmine. Jasmine prodded it experimentally. It felt lumpy, and it crackled in a plastic-sounding way.

Bursting with curiosity, Jasmine tore off the snowman paper. Underneath was a pink plastic

sack. The black writing said: PIG STARTER AND GROWER PELLETS.

"Food for Truffle! Thank you, Manu. That's really kind of you."

Manu was still bouncing up and down on his chair. "Now give her your present!" he said, looking eagerly at Dad.

Dad glanced toward the door. "Jasmine, this is from Mom and me," he said. "We hope you'll like it."

Everybody turned to the door. Jasmine heard a familiar grunt. In walked Mom, with a huge smile on her face, and beside her, gleaming with cleanliness and wearing a big red bow around her neck, was Truffle.

Jasmine stared in confusion. Everyone was grinning at her. But Truffle was already hers. How could she be a Christmas present?

Dad smiled at her. "Jasmine, I know I said I don't keep pigs and we weren't going to keep Truffle. But you've proven that pigs have a lot more to them than I've ever given them credit for. And

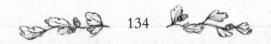

134

you've also proven yourself as a top pig keeper. So how would you like to keep Truffle here?"

Jasmine stared at her father. "Forever?"

"Yes. Forever. Provided she behaves herself, of course."

Truffle trotted over to Jasmine, grunting her contented grunt. Jasmine knelt on the fireside rug, scooped up her piglet, and clasped her in a huge hug.

"So what do you think, Jas?" asked Mom. "It's an unusual sort of present, I know, but we thought you might like it."

Jasmine sat up on the rug and grinned at her parents. "Thank you so, so much," she said. "I like it more than anything else in the whole entire world."

Turn the page for
an interview with Jasmine and
a sneak peek of the next book in the
JASMINE GREEN RESCUES series!

A Q&A with Jasmine Green

What do you do when you meet a new animal for the first time?

That's a hard question to answer because every animal is different. Some, like puppies and kittens, are usually friendly with humans. Wild animals tend to be much more wary of people. I would only approach a wild animal if it needed help — if it was injured or trapped, for example. Even then, I would be really careful to avoid its teeth and claws! If I didn't know the animal, and it didn't need urgent attention, I would just watch it from a distance to see how it acted. If it seemed calm, I would speak softly to it and try to be friendly. You can usually tell by an animal's reaction whether it wants to be near humans: if it growled, bared its teeth, or moved away, I would keep my distance!

What's it like living on a farm?

It's great! There are always animals to care for and spend time with. My favorite time of year is spring, because that's when the lambs are born. There are always a few that need extra feeding from a bottle, or even need to be hand-reared. Lambs are so cute, and if you hand-rear a lamb, it bonds with you forever. The ones I fed years ago still remember me and run to greet me when I come into their field. The other thing that's great about living on a farm is that there's so much space. My best friend, Tom, and I love making tree houses and dens in the fields and woods, and it's always easy to discover a new place to build.

How did you meet Toffee and Marmite?

I first saw Toffee and Marmite at a local animal shelter. Their owner had moved and couldn't take them with her, so they needed a new home. When I walked toward their cage, they ran to greet me.

They stood on their back legs with their paws up against the wire, gazing at me with pleading looks. I knew they wanted me to take them home. I had to persuade my mom to let me have two cats, but Toffee and Marmite are siblings and had always lived together. It wouldn't have been right to separate them. And it's really nice that there are two of them, because they're best friends. They always sleep cuddled together with their front paws touching, like they're holding hands!

How many animals do you have now?

I have Toffee and Marmite, and my newest pet, Truffle the pig! She was tiny when I rescued her, but she's grown really fast. By the time she's finished growing, she'll be enormous! Luckily, we have plenty of space on the farm. She loves living in the orchard and sharing a kennel with my dad's spaniel, Bramble. They became friends when Truffle was a baby, and now they're best friends for life. It's so cute to see them running around in the orchard together.

Jasmine Green Rescues

Rescues

A Duckling
Called Button

1
Put That Down!

"Good girl, Truffle," said Jasmine, bending down to scratch her pig behind the ears. "Good girl."

Jasmine and her best friend, Tom, were walking Truffle around the edge of the biggest field on Oak Tree Farm, checking Jasmine's dad's flock of Southdown sheep. It was a lovely warm March morning. The sky was a beautiful pale blue, with high, fluffy clouds.

The sheep were due to lamb next month, and they had to be checked twice a day to make sure they were all right. Jasmine always took Truffle with her on these walks. She had rescued the pig from another farm, as a tiny newborn runt, and nursed her back to health. Now four months old, Truffle lived happily in the orchard next to the farmhouse, but she loved to go for walks with Jasmine.

"That sheep's stuck," said Tom, pointing toward the bottom of the field. A ewe lay upside down, arching her back and kicking her legs in the air, trying to get onto her feet.

The children walked quickly toward the sheep, Truffle trotting beside them.

"She must have rolled over to rub an itchy patch," said Jasmine. "She's too heavy in lamb to get up again, poor thing."

When they reached the stuck sheep, Jasmine said, "Sit, Truffle." Truffle sat obediently while Jasmine and Tom crouched beside the ewe.

"Let's get you back on your feet," Jasmine said. "We don't want a fox or a badger attacking you, do we?"

They placed their hands under the ewe's side and heaved her up. She scrambled to her feet and trotted off without a backward glance. Jasmine watched her happily. But Tom was frowning.

"There's a dog over there. Down by the river."

The far side of the meadow bordered the river. Trees and bushes grew along the banks. Some sheep had been grazing peacefully there, but now they started running across the field, baaing in panic.

Jasmine saw a flash of brown among the bushes.

"Off the leash, in a field full of sheep," she said. "It must be a stray. You run and get my dad. I'll stay here to chase it away if it tries to attack the ewes."

"Ugh," said Tom. "Look. I bet it's hers."

A girl in purple boots and a black coat with a fur-trimmed hood was walking along the public footpath that ran across the fields by the river. Somebody Jasmine and Tom knew all too well: Bella Bradley, the most annoying girl in their class.

Fury surged through Jasmine. She grabbed Truffle's leash and marched over to the girl.

"Bella Bradley! Is that your dog?"

Bella barely glanced at Jasmine. "Duh," she said. "Who else's dog would it be? I don't see anyone else around here."

"Well, you need to put it on a leash."

"Why should I?"

"Because these sheep are all in lamb. If your dog chases them, they could lose their lambs."

"My dog doesn't chase sheep. And you can't tell me what to do."

She strode off across the field.

Jasmine, boiling with rage, was about to retort when a tremendous squawking and beating of wings came from the direction of the river. She turned to see what was going on.

Bella's terrier shot out from the bushes. In its

mouth was a duck, flapping its wings and quacking frantically.

"Hey!" shouted Jasmine. "Put that down!"

She and Tom raced across the field after the dog, the duck clamped in its jaws. Tom picked up a clod of earth and hurled it at the terrier, but it missed.

When it reached the hedge, the dog dropped the duck and squeezed into the hedgerow. Jasmine and Tom fell to their knees beside the duck. It was a female mallard. Jasmine placed her hands on the soft, warm underbody.

There was no movement beneath her feathers. No heartbeat.

"She's dead," said Jasmine. "That dog killed her."

Jasmine Green Rescues

A Piglet
Called Truffle

Helen Peters

Illustrated by Ellie Snowdon

WALKER BOOKS

Jasmine Green Rescues

A Duckling
Called Button

Helen Peters

Illustrated by Ellie Snowdon

WALKER BOOKS

Jasmine Green Rescues

A Lamb
Called Lucky

Helen Peters

Illustrated by Ellie Snowdon

WALKER BOOKS

Jasmine Green Rescues

A Goat
Called Willow

Helen Peters

Illustrated by Ellie Snowdon

WALKER BOOKS

Which animals have you helped Jasmine rescue?

☐ A Piglet Called Truffle

☐ A Duckling Called Button

☐ A Collie Called Sky

☐ A Kitten Called Holly

☐ A Lamb Called Lucky

☐ A Goat Called Willow

About the Creators

Helen Peters is the author of numerous books for young readers that feature heroic girls saving the day on farms. She grew up on an old-fashioned farm in England, surrounded by family, animals, and mud. Helen Peters lives in London.

Ellie Snowdon is a children's author-illustrator from a tiny village in South Wales. She received her MA in children's book illustration at Cambridge School of Art. Ellie Snowdon lives in Cambridge, England.